THE RACE TO PEARL PEAK

A Popeye Adventure

by Edith T. Kunhardt • illustrated by Manny Campana

Golden Press • New York
Western Publishing Company, Inc. Racine, Wisconsin

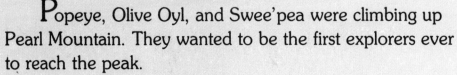

Popeye, Olive Oyl, and Swee'pea were climbing up Pearl Mountain. They wanted to be the first explorers ever to reach the peak.

"Pretty soon—*puff, puff*—our flag will be flying from the top of Pearl Peak—*puff, puff*—and we'll be famous," Popeye said. "Maybe they'll even change its name to Mount Popeye!"

"Oh, Popeye, how thrilling," said Olive Oyl, hauling herself around a boulder. "Look, I see ice and snow up ahead."

"Avast, Olive, that means we're getting near the top," Popeye said. "Let's stop here and put on our ice equipment."

They sat down and strapped crampons onto
their boots so they wouldn't slide on the ice.
They put on gloves and parkas to keep warm.
Then they put on their backpacks, grabbed their
ice axes, and began to climb again.

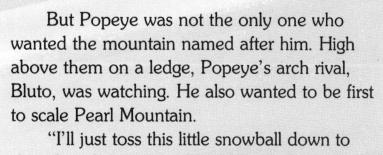

But Popeye was not the only one who
wanted the mountain named after him. High
above them on a ledge, Popeye's arch rival,
Bluto, was watching. He also wanted to be first
to scale Pearl Mountain.

"I'll just toss this little snowball down to
slow them," he said. "Then I'll win the race
to the top. Ha, ha, ha!"

Bluto's snowball landed far uphill from Popeye, Swee'pea, and Olive. But as it rolled down it gathered more snow and began to grow. It grew and grew—until it was gigantic.

Closer and closer the huge snowball bounded, racing right toward Popeye, Olive, and Swee'pea.

"Popeye, help! Save us!" screamed Olive.

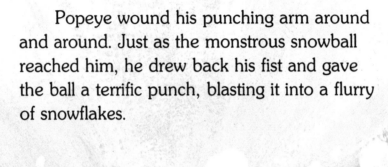

Popeye wound his punching arm around
and around. Just as the monstrous snowball
reached him, he drew back his fist and gave
the ball a terrific punch, blasting it into a flurry
of snowflakes.

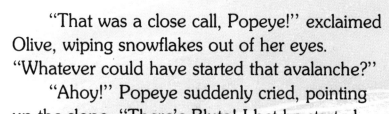

"That was a close call, Popeye!" exclaimed
Olive, wiping snowflakes out of her eyes.
"Whatever could have started that avalanche?"

"Ahoy!" Popeye suddenly cried, pointing
up the slope. "There's Bluto! I bet he started
that avalanche so *he* could beat us to the top.
But we're not going to let him get there first.
Let's go!"

They struck off across a big ice field, racing after Bluto.

Bluto stayed well ahead of them, climbing higher and higher and never letting them catch up. When he reached the top of a slope, he turned and bellowed, "You'll never catch me!"

"Catch me…catch me…catch me!"
Bluto's booming voice echoed back and forth
among the hills. And then…

...he stepped back and plunged into a deep crevasse.

"Blimey!" crowed Popeye. "He's dropped out of the race!"

"No! No! He's in trouble! You've got to save him, Popeye!" Olive Oyl begged.

On hands and knees they crawled to the edge of the crevasse and peered down. There was Bluto, hanging by his pack strap in the jagged blue crack.

"Help!" he cried, beginning to sob. "Please help me! I'll never bother you again, ever!"

"Here, Popeye," cried Olive. "Here are some special bars of dried spinach. I brought them along for energy!"

"Oh, all right," said Popeye, wolfing down the spinach bars. "I hate wasting spinach on Bluto. But I am what I am and I'll do me duty!"

Strength flowed into Popeye's muscles.
He seemed to grow taller and wider. His chest
swelled out. His parka strained at the seams.

Then with a flurry of his ice ax and a shower of ice slivers, Popeye chopped a stairway in the ice right down to Bluto. He unhooked the pack strap and carried Bluto up the steps.

"Thanks, pal. I'll always be grateful to you," said Bluto. "At least until we reach the top," he added, under his breath.

"Now, boys, no more fighting," said Olive. "And no more races! Let's all climb this mountain together."

They roped themselves together
and started up once more. Just before
they reached the summit they came to
a steep cliff.

Popeye inched his way up,
hammering pitons into the slippery ice
to use as handholds and footholds.

When he reached the top of the
cliff, he hammered in a belaying pin
and anchored himself to it by his rope.
Then he hauled the others up.

"Greetings, friends," said a voice from the summit. "Come and join me in a delicious repast."

Everyone stopped short.

"Am I dreaming?" cried Olive.

It was Popeye's friend Wimpy. He had set up his hamburger stand right on the very top of Pearl Peak.

"Blimey!" exclaimed Popeye, staring at Wimpy.
"How did *you* get here?"

"I climbed up the other side," Wimpy replied.

"Well, shiver me timbers," said Popeye,
chewing on his pipe.

"Never mind, Popeye," said Olive. "What counts is that we're all here. Let's plant our flag and celebrate."

And so they did.